AF326785

PASCHIA'S HIDDEN JOURNALS

VOL. 1: AWAKENINGS & AEVEATERNITY

AN ELEMENTS OF TIME STORY BY

SAM PAISLEY

First Edition:
ISBN: 978-1-7390400-5-5 (Hardcover)
ISBN: 978-1-7390400-9-3 (Paperback)
ISBN: 978-1-7390400-7-9 (eBook)
ISBN: 978-1-7390400-6-2 (Audiobook)

Cover Art & Design: Seventhstar Art
Interior Design: Adrian M. Gibson

Like the story? You can find out more about the series, artwork, merchandise and more at www.elementsoftime.ca

This book is dedicated to my wonderful wife, and to my daughter on the way. The former has the patience to allow me to pursue my passion, and the latter is the reason I pursue it. To my daughter—I hope to share these stories with you one day, and to build worlds for you as wonderful as the life I hope you have.

A note, to you

I am not surprised that you have found these journals. If you have sought out my writing, the inevitable has happened.

I share with you now these accounts, neither to garner pity nor praise, but so you have a reference by which to make your own decisions.

I am entrusting you with secrets that none other than myself have yet to discover, knowledge that speaks to the very nature of creation itself.

More than anyone else, you understood that my life was one obsessed with the art of bringing forth the yet to be imagined, and turning possibility into reality. This, of course, is the joy of an inventor—to solve the mysteries that other minds have yet to conceive.

If you are in fact reading my words now, you are no doubt searching for answers. In these writings you will find some, but not all. You know me well enough to know I would not be so reckless as to keep my most guarded treasures in one place.

What I provide for you here is a key, the first step in a long journey— one that you must choose to walk of your own accord. The power of what I have learned is nearly unparalleled, though, even despite my own fate, I could not bring myself to simply destroy it. I trust only you with the secrets I have hidden. If you so choose, my work is yours to find and to protect. For power is simply the form that knowledge takes.

Aeveaternity 1

I am awakened.

I have opened my eyes. Or, no, Father has given me eyes to open.

I think, but I do not know how.

Where I am, my existence. This realm, it is…without form. It is all. I am one with all.

Aeveaternity II

I have heard Father's voice. He is pure, he is all. He has given me life, created everything I exist within. He says that this realm is one of Time, that I am a child of Time. I do not understand what that means.

I can feel myself at once as part of all. I wish to understand who… what…

I… am

How can I be?

Aeveaternity III

Father has created others like me. Brothers and sisters. He has called us the Aevea, and this place Aeveaternity.

I yearn to meet them, and yet, I feel as though I already have, that I am a part of them and them a part of me. He has a plan for us, this much I've known since awakening. Perhaps. Perhaps that is what he means when he says I am a being of Time. All, and one. Distinct, yet infinite.

I… it is a mystery. So much knowledge to gain. A challenge I am eager to conquer.

For now, and for always, I know. I am not alone—I never was, and never can be.

Form to Potential I

A question has taken shape in my mind. I believe it similarly haunts my brothers and sisters. What is my purpose?

Father has given me and my siblings yet another gift. He has given us all names, and with those names a role, a responsibility.

Father has named me Paschia: He Who Forms Potential. And yet, I am not sure what this means.

What does it mean to form potential? I am not certain I understand either term: form or potential.

All things that have ever existed and will ever exist have already come to be. Is that not what it means to be in Aeveaternity, to be in Father's domain? What, then, does Father mean when he describes potential?

And form, what does it mean for something to have form? I do not have a form as far as I know. If that is the case, then why do I exist? Why has he named me such, and imbued me with a curiosity for answers that do not yet have questions?

He has told me that I have within me the ability to shape that which we do not yet know. While I cannot create something new, something outside of him, he has told me I am capable of taking his materials and *building* something novel.

I do not know what it means to build, but I trust Father. I trust that he understands more than I will ever know. I trust that there is a part of me that can do what he believes me able to do.

Perhaps that is my purpose. Perhaps that is the meaning of my name. Perhaps that is potential.

I trust Father.

What is poten What must I do?

The Aevea 1

ather has blessed me and my siblings with so many gifts. I admire them all so deeply.

Dignis is noble, he inspires virtue in everything he touches.

Raysh Io is reason beyond compare, the logic of the universe itself; his role within Father's perfect tapestry is self-evident.

Serenya's gifts extend beyond words, for she and she alone can exert the elegant guidance necessary for Father's will.

My dear, sweet brother Viserum sees the beauty in Father's creations. His abilities are perhaps the purest of us all.

I could happily spend my existence speaking to the glories of my brothers and sisters, but that would be betraying the gifts that Father has bestowed upon me.

Though I do not yet understand the depth of this duty, it is one I intend to fulfill.

The Second Realm 1

Father has created something of true magnificence. It is greater than even my wildest imaginings. Words, something I am gaining a growing appreciation for, cannot describe the sophistication and intricacy of Father's work. He has created more than Time, from nothing created something.

Father has created a Second Realm.

I see now what it means to have form. I have so much to learn, so many questions to ask. I feel as though my mind has opened in a way unthinkable only moments ago.

I am in awe. I understand now, I have a duty to this place, a duty to Father.

Remember this moment.

Remember what Father

has created.

A second realm.

The Aevea II

Dolour is wise, I've known this since before I've known him. Seeing him, speaking with him, I understand my own self more. My awareness has given shape to my form, and the more aware I become, the more my own form is defined.

Dolour has noted my unique tendency to record my thoughts. This is a habit I myself have not consciously realized I was doing, or perhaps had not realized was unique.

As we are beings of infinite Time, to record our thoughts is to give them permanence, to give them form—a body—in a way that infinity cannot. By recording thought, it becomes memory, and memory becomes history. Have I already been doing this? I know all of my thoughts since my awakening as if they were happening in this moment. Yet, to record them is an act beyond knowing. Recording is an act of separation, of isolation, and, therefore, of making whole.

Again, I ask myself, have I already been doing this? It is difficult to tell in a realm of pure Time…

I know that I have put my thoughts into physical form, journals which hold important moments of recollection since the dawn of my existence. Whether or not this action begot my own form, or whether the opposite is true, is difficult to tell. However, since Father created the Second Realm, I have sensed a change within myself, one that I believe to be important enough to capture. By recording in writing what has come before, I can be certain that my knowledge has form.

Dolour seems to have noticed this change in my nature before even I could. He seems to understand myself and our siblings in a way that the rest of us simply do not, or cannot. I believe his instinct in noting this habit will prove to be an astute observation, though for what purpose I cannot fathom.

Father says that Dolour is the embodiment of something that is yet to be, and that his gifts are ones that will extend beyond us and between us. I do not know what Father means by this, but I have learned from knowing Dolour, that he is different than I am. He has knowledge of something I have not yet experienced—he appears to know what it means to end.

To end...

*Is it possible
to learn what
Dolour knows?*

The Second Realm 11

I have become enraptured in studying the Second Realm, and, in doing so, have discovered so many things.

Father says that this realm, adjacent to our own but outside of it, is a realm of Space and Time, together. As a being of Time, I do not yet understand this distinction, but I have found an enormous amount of clarity knowing a distinction exists.

There is a linearity that occurs in the Second Realm. It appears to function causally: one action begets another, which begets another. From that, you can, with great accuracy, predict the outcome of any given event, or series of events. My brother Raysh Io has proven particularly skilled at understanding linearity, cause and effect; this talent seems to be part of the gifts that Father has bestowed upon him. I will make it a priority to study with him for a time, to try to learn this skill.

Until laying eyes upon this new realm, learning this concept of 'Space', I had been unable to comprehend what Father has meant me to do. In our realm, we existed, and have always existed, at all points at once, disperse, and yet whole. Form, embodiment, these were but abstractions without the contrast.

Space is the contrast to Time. They both give the other clarity, acting as mirrors, if not companions to one another.

I am determined to learn more. I believe the relationship between Space and Time will allow me to understand what is meant by potential. Then, with luck, I will know my own purpose for existing.

The Aevea III

To quote my brother, Viserum:

"It is my duty to observe, and nothing more. For simply observing is an action enough to change the course of events. Observation is the highest of actions; the untold and infinite beauty of the universe deserves nothing less than to be appreciated."

Viserum has been given a great gift by Father, one that he relishes and abides by with the utmost solemnity.

I have studied how he interacts with our siblings. The way that he looks at us, the way that he looks at our realm, I am curious if I might ever understand what he sees. He seems to know things, yet not have words for them. He describes our forms, and essences, but cannot tell us what that means to him beyond vague talk of colours and light.

The Second Realm III

Whether they will admit it or not, I can tell my brothers and sisters understand themselves better in relation to the Second Realm than they did before its creation. Father had given us life, given us duties, but no domain in which to express those duties. We were but infants, playing at responsibility, without any sense of reality beyond what was immediately before us. There was no true depth to this way of thinking.

I have seen my siblings' abilities come to life in new and invigorating ways as they have explored their relationship with causality. Father's guidance in this manner has allowed us all to experience complexities and profundities greater than we have ever known.

The kind Serenya has proven exceedingly adept at guiding events in the Second Realm with intricate tact that astounds us all.

As always, Dolour understands a depth beyond any of our ken.

And Dignis, great, noble Dignis, has aligned us all under a proper orientation toward Father's will. Through him we understand clearly our duty, and can interpret our place amongst all things.

Form to Potential 11

I have learned much by studying the Second Realm. There is a power there that does not exist here. I have consulted with Dolour, who appears to appreciate this power better than anyone. He refers to this power using the term '*limitations*'. The irony, as he points out, is that a limitation definitionally binds the infinite; it creates the finite, and, in doing so, creates truer meaning.

I, as a being of Time, do not understand what it means to be anything other than infinite, though it is an area I intend to study with great diligence.

Limitations... Can there be form without the finite? Can I exist without the finite? Can I exist within it?

The Aevea IV

I did not believe it possible, but Viserum is more captivated by the Second Realm than even myself. He said that the beauty contained there is like nothing Father has created before. His exuberance for the inestimable mix of chaos and order is outmatched only by his fervour to see it all.

How does one, even a being of Aeveaternity, see all of the ever-expanding shape of existence? We, of course, have the benefit of unlimited time, but how does that compare to a realm of immeasurable and intertwined Space and Time?

It is a paradox of self, of purpose, of meaning. It is yet another seemingly unreachable goal, a challenge that in itself gives the goal value.

I do not believe Father created us and gave us purpose simply so that we may never achieve it.

My strength seems to lie in study, and gathering knowledge. Perhaps my purpose then is to use that knowledge to forge tools that will aid my brothers and sisters in pursuing their goals.

I have been reflecting on limitations. My duty to Father is to form potential. I have come to believe that there can be no potential without limitations. Even more so, without limitations, potential has no value whatsoever.

Potential is infinite, yet form is finite. It is a contradiction in terms, but one that Father has so perfectly solved in the Second Realm. I could never have realized this without the assistance and tutelage of my siblings. I understand now that I have within me the ability to craft extensions of myself and my siblings, objects that can amplify their natural gifts and affinities.

Much like this process of recording my thoughts, I shall attempt to move potential, the infinite, through the lens of the finite, and give shape to something new. It is not true creation of course, for that is a power that only Father will ever possess. But, this gift, this ability that Father has given to me, is, in a deeply ironic sense, one of limitless potential.

I have found that aiding my brothers and sisters is a deeply fulfilling way to serve Father.

The Second Realm is a beautiful burden. It is at once a gift that has allowed all of us a depth of meaning beyond what we could have ever dreamed. And yet, I can see how its care affects my siblings.

The Second Realm is ever expanding, ever changing and growing. For beings such as ourselves, to face a realm so far outside our own fundamental essence is daunting. It is a challenge that we take on with dutiful fervor, but a challenge nonetheless.

In my continued study of the Second Realm, I have learned more about my own abilities than in all of the time before its creation. The more I learn, the more I realize I have always had this knowledge, and yet, have never had it. The process of gaining knowledge feels as though I have accessed a memory that I had not known had been hidden, then suddenly becomes almost self-evident. This is the paradoxical curse and gift of being a child of Time.

At the moment, I am experimenting on a tool that will help my dear brother, Viserum. He is called and compelled to observe, in great detail, the Second Realm.

Father has blessed Viserum with the gift of sight, and an appreciation of beauty in a way the rest of us will never know. Perhaps that is why he seems different from us—like Dolour, but somehow the opposite.

It is frustrating; I feel as though I do not yet have the language to properly articulate what my mind already knows. However, acquiring language is simply yet another opportunity to form the potential that exists within me, and gives all the more import to each of these entries.

Knowledge. Language. Memory. They are connected.

The Aevea

I have completed my work on the device to help Viserum—an elegant creation, and one that I am proud to share with my brother.

It is strange for any being of Aeveaternity to interact with a realm of linear causality. We exist at all points in time, yet Viserum, by his nature, must look at the universe as it is happening. This strain causes him duress, an incongruence that I hope my new invention will alleviate.

With this device, Viserum will be able to channel his power to see any point in the Second Realm that he desires, while safely staying within the bounds of our own realm. It will create a necessary divide from the effects of the Second Realm, while channeling and amplifying his abilities within our own.

My siblings and I are constantly growing and changing from the influence of Father's Second Realm. There is discomfort in this. Despite our truest of loyalties, I know that for some it feels counter to their very nature to interact with a realm so heavily comprised of Space.

I believe it to be my responsibility to forge tools to mitigate this discomfort, so that we all may better serve in our stewardship. What more noble purpose could one have than to aid his kind in their solemn duty?

Form to Potential

To my surprise, I have discovered that I have grown a remarkable affinity to that which I give form. Though they are but mere objects, the eventuality of focused potential, I cannot help but feel connected to them. The effort and care that goes into every invention that I craft imbues them, in a way, with part of my essence. While I know this is simply metaphorical, I have begun to suspect, on occasion, my inventions feel this connection as well.

Dolour has recommended a novel idea. He has wisely pointed out that Father's first act upon creating myself and my siblings was to give us all names.

As I have reflected on his words, I have realized that it is quite similar to the first piece of advice that Dolour had ever given me. Under his guidance I began recording my thoughts, and in doing so, those thoughts became memory; they became distinct and gained a nature of their own. Through memory, I became more than an infinite being existing across all of Time. I became a singular line across Aeveaternity—a small distinction, but an important one nonetheless.

In many ways, the power of language is similar to my own abilities. Language gives form, real, tangible form, to thought. And I give form to potential. What is the difference between thought and potential? Perhaps nothing at all.

A name. Just as Father did, I will ensure that to which I give form—my children—I shall name.

The Sentients 1

I have not known the depths of potential, nor what it means to capture it, until now. It shames me to think how juvenile my work has been to this point, to think I considered myself remotely learned of the mysteries of the universe.

Father has created something new.

In the Second Realm, Father has formed creatures endowed with but a spark of his purity, and an unbreakable connection to our plane of existence. That connection is so profound, that Serenya can even touch it from within the Aeveaternity.

These beings are unique, ever-changing, and so fragile. Compared to us, their connection to Father seems so insignificant, so removed. And yet, I sense something within them that fills me with great hope.

Viserum has said that when he looks at these creatures, he can see the infinitely intricate overlap of who they are and who they can become in a beautiful cacophony of ever-changing colour. The same, he says, cannot be said of our kind—we are, and have always been, but a single, purely defined colour in even our deepest essence. He says, however, that our colours shine much brighter than these new beings ever will. I may never understand exactly how Viserum sees the universe, but I do have an inkling as to what he might be referring to regarding these inhabitants of the Second Realm.

These beings of the Second Realm, they are but infants in their awareness. They barely have enough lifespan to even contemplate what Father has created for them. However, unlike us, this limited life produces within them limitless potential. While their incarnate lives may be short, they have will, they have choice, and they will struggle because of it. And it will be the act of striving beyond those limits, and forging a path completely their own, that will be Father's greatest gift to them.

The Aevea Io

My sister, Serenya, is one of the most caring individuals the universe may ever know. She concerns herself with the well-being of *all* things, so much that she can even *touch* the ceaselessly complex tendrils of Father's Second Realm. She innately understands how the fabric of that universe is connected to itself, and to us.

In a way that I have yet to comprehend, Serenya is able to see the movement of causality itself. She understands on an intimate level how Space can and will move through Time. This is different than Raysh Io's explanation of cause and effect, as her perspective is based far more on creating ideal outcomes than merely dealing in actualities.

The more I study under my siblings, the more I realize how much I have yet to learn. Each one presents me with entirely new frontiers of knowledge. I am constantly humbled by my brothers and sisters, none more so than kind Serenya.

She is able to touch so many things, to focus on the ever-expanding possibilities of the Second Realm, all while possessing such admirable grace.

I can only imagine the toll the magnitude of her responsibility must take on her.

This is why I must continue to study with my brethren. I do not simply yearn for knowledge, though that much is true as well. I hope that by so passionately observing my brothers and sisters that I may continue to develop tools to ease their unspoken and willing burdens.

The burden of knowledge.
It is too important to disavow.
I must continue to learn.

Form to Potential 01

It brings me endless joy giving form to tools that are put to good use. And while I deeply admire my siblings, none are more capable or interested in exploring the uses of my inventions than the Sentients. These beings have a creativity and imagination that is actually *bolstered* by the limitations of their realm.

At first, I believed the notion that my tools could feel or connect with their users to be absurd. However, the more of them I produce, and the more they are used by the Sentients, the more I can sense my tools reaching out to bond with those around them. As such, I have decided to label my inventions 'empathic.' I know they do not truly think, for they do not have minds. However, I also know that they do act differently depending on the user. From this I can only assume that one does not need to be able to think in order to feel.

I strive to create as many useful tools as I can. I am fascinated by what is possible, and duty bound by discovery. However, though my creativity is vast, it is dwarfed by the combined and ever-expanding curiosity of the Sentients.

Just as their lives begin embryonically, I've created, what could be considered, an embryo for empathic tools—a seed of pure potential, to be imprinted upon and molded with the memories and personality of its wielder. Like how the stars, with their tremendous power, appear as pinpoints in the night's sky, the embryos of my inventions are nothing more than simple beads of brilliant light.

I have witnessed what has happened when a deserving Sentient grasps one of these embryos. The result is not only remarkable, but joyous to behold. These two pure forms of potential bond to one another; they touch each other's innermost souls and become intertwined.

My siblings and I were created with the specific purpose to aid Father in his ambitions. As such, my children were created as perfect means to help Sentients in their ambitions, should they be deserving enough to reach for them.

There is a risk in this path, however. In my fervour and arrogance, I have not been cautious enough. I have witnessed the result when an undeserving Sentient grasps one of these seeds. If the heart is impure, or the intent malicious, my empathic tools can be used for terrible purposes. As a steward of the Second Realm, I will not be a harbinger of destruction amongst its inhabitants. Though I am tremendously excited by the possibilities of these empathic embryos, I must not be reckless with when and how they are given to the Sentients.

Absence 1

I hesitate to put these words onto the page, as to immortalize them in memory.

None of us can find Father.

Though his disappearance was subtle, his absence leaves us with an implacable hollowness. Of course, if he has left us, or hidden himself from us in some way, it is by intention. I know him to be wise enough to have good reason for any action he takes, and my siblings share the same resolve.

We shall all continue our work with the utmost diligence until he returns.

Where is Father?

*Can one such as he
simply disappear?*

The Aevea oll

I asked Serenya how she could possibly manage the chaos of infinity in a realm where Time moves so rigidly, and Space creates boundaries. Her words were illuminating. She has such clear sense about her, such clear purpose. Perhaps that has much to do with her abilities, with the gift of piecing together disparate threads to make things whole.

Her zeal inspires me. In these trying times I have come to rely more on my siblings than ever before. Though none can replace Father, I have found comfort in the camaraderie of my kin.

For fear that I may not remember her words, I will document them here, a habit of which I have come to rely upon.

"Before the Sentients, the Second Realm was simple. Every atom travelled as an individual, weaving in intricacies that were miraculous and marvelous, yet predictable. I learned this causal nature, and understood how to direct it to produce the most wonderous beauty of patterns and symmetry. In contrast, our realm, where we live in blissful Aeveaternity, is perfectly stable, and such the patterns and symmetry are already complete.

"The Sentients brought with them an interesting, if not unforeseen, challenge for me. Their reason for being, as far as I can understand, much like the stars from which they are made, is to combine, reproduce, and eventually perish. In this way, they give their bodies back to the Second Realm so that more of them may be created. However, Father did more than give them form. He bestowed within them a spark of himself, and, possibly, a piece of each of us. He connected them intimately to our realm of Aeveaternity, and simultaneously bestowed within their nature a deep connection to Space itself. As such, their blended nature means that they also contain an element of chaos.

"The beautiful creatures they are, they struggle and strive to constantly find 'meaning'. If they achieve it, they strive for more. They are like us, in a way; however, unlike us, they will never be satisfied in the work that they do. If you hand them what they want, or even need, they reject it outright. Unlike stars, with the Sentients I cannot simply place an atom where it needs to be for

a reaction to occur. Sentients require the most delicate of touch; they require subtlety. Father gave them will, which means they must believe their choices are their own. Their triumphs and their failures, their successes and challenges must be of their own doing in order to have any lasting meaning to them. My purpose is only to provide guidance, and that is all I am truly capable of doing. Their bodies, their lives, though infinitesimally short, contain so much more than they could ever fully understand. Their threads are incredibly robust.

"It is my greatest joy, and greatest challenge, weaving the tapestry of the Sentients. Although the complexity is demanding, sometimes maddeningly so, I would not wish for my duty to be any different. I know that, through this charge, I am serving Father's greatest of purposes. Maybe I have become too close to the Sentients, and their willful determination has infected me. Bless them for that, if that is the case."

She is so strong in Father's absence. She has only become more committed to her duty.

I have so enjoyed studying her ways. I look forward to the day where my tools will help her complete her work.

The Aevea VIII

Ican see the sorrow growing in Viserum as he is forced to watch the Sentients, for which he cares so deeply, grow old and perish. Although they share a tether to our realm even after death, this connection is not as strong as the one Viserum shares with them when they are embodied in the Second Realm.

He has learned, with practice, that by sharing his gift with the Sentients, he can appreciate much more of the Second Realm than through his eyes alone. He has imbued part of himself into their vision, and in many ways has become more like them in exchange. It has given him tremendous joy, and yet, perhaps an equal amount of anguish.

Countless Sentients are conceived every moment, and countless perish at the same time. Their lives are so linear, and so bitterly short. I understand that it is the limited nature of their being that makes them wonderfully appreciative of beauty, yet the pain of their ending stays with Viserum.

Much like many of my siblings, he has been touched in a most profound way by the Sentients and their realm. Like all of us, Viserum believes that sharing his gift is crucial to the role for which Father has created him. However, I fear the pain of the endless loss, of their short and fragile lives, is a weight that grows too heavy for Viserum to bear.

The Sentients who follow him and directly borrow his gift, The Gaze, live lives of incredible, quiet beauty. They give a tremendous gift back to Viserum—even more eyes through which to experience Father's magnificence. I only wish that this exchange did not come at the cost of Viserum's spirit.

Joy and pain...

Can beauty exist without sacrifice?

Eleva Prime 1

I am admittedly impressed; Viserum has surpassed even my abilities. Although I have devoted my existence to giving form to ideas, what Viserum has done goes far beyond what I would have ever considered possible.

I am, in this moment, at a loss for words. And yet, I know it necessary to document this occasion to the degree to which I am able.

I do not entirely understand the method by which she came to be, though I do know that, in all of the universe, she is unique. Viserum has somehow created a bridge between the Second Realm and our own that I did not know *could* exist.

I have hypotheses as to how this occurred, most of which center around Viserum's unique relationship with the Second Realm and the Sentients themselves. Though I have no evidence to corroborate this theory, I have a suspicion that whatever allowed this miracle to occur would be incredibly difficult, but not necessarily impossible, to repeat.

I am not certain how my brothers and sisters will feel about her; most of them are so occupied in their own work that it likely would not dawn on them to care. More to the point, in the limited amount of time I have been able to spend with her, I have been utterly captivated by her.

Whether it is the sheer novelty of her existence, her intellect, or her curiosity in my work, I adore my niece, Calara Voya. She is the first and only of her kind—the daughter of an Aevea. Viserum's progeny. An Eleva Prime.

Absence II

It has been a painful amount of time without Father's presence. Our duties keep us bound to the Second Realm, which makes all of us increasingly aware of the slow and linear passage of time.

I toil in my work with an increased fervor every moment he is not with us. At times I feel as though my work is the only thing that keeps me connected to him. And other times it feels like endless punishment, as I strive to achieve an obligation that can never be satisfied.

I have heard whispers of fear that he might not return, however, I remain hopeful. Though it has been difficult, his continued presence is clear for those paying proper attention.

The last instruction any of us recall hearing from him was: "Our duty is to maintain balance."

Before Father's absence, balance had never been defined, nor had it been our objective. However, we all know ourselves to be Father's stewards. It is our responsibility to care for what he has directed us to care for, and to do so dutifully until his inevitable return.

I am coming to believe that this duty, more than anything else, is the reason for our combined existence.

Fear. Duty. Balance.
His presence is clear
with proper attention.

Absence III

I write now with a renewed resilience and vigour. Just as we had begun to waiver in our conviction, Dignis has proven his exemplary ability to lead. He has seen our individual struggles and united us once again, not simply as custodians of our individual domains, but as brothers and sisters unified in devotion to serve Father's final command.

I can say this with the utmost clarity: Dignis is the greatest among us. He is will and purity incarnate, more fervent and devout to Father than anyone. His strength emanates to everything around him, not unlike Father's did, though Dignis himself would be the first to shudder at such a comparison. In aspiring to follow Dignis, I believe I might have gleaned an understanding of how Viserum sees reality. Dignis exudes a golden nature—a colour whose power I have come to appreciate in my own work.

Dignis' is certain of Father's return, and his certainty has spread to us all. I have not seen my siblings so diligent in their pursuits since Father's absence.

The Elevated I

After countless eons of observing the Second Realm, Dignis has come to believe he has solved Father's final request. He sees within the Sentients a goodness and potential to be more than they are: to be like us. Dignis feels that the balance that Father spoke of is one where all may live in the unchanging and perfect form of the Aevea—one where all potential is reality, and all reality potential.

In Dignis's judgment, it is our mission to 'elevate' the Sentients to grow beyond their mortal nature and become as we are. Though my brothers and sisters have found different ways to try to accomplish this goal, I firmly believe that providing the Sentients with the correct tools is the best way to aid them in Elevation.

We have seen the effect that tools have on countless Sentient species across the entirety of the Second Realm. The advent of tools is typically one of the earliest signs that a species will gain, if not has already gained, true Sentience. It is unquestionable that as Sentients master tools, they begin to master themselves, which, I believe, makes them increasingly akin to us.

In studying the countless Sentient societies across the Second Realm, I have noticed that means of transportation are almost always an analog for their advancement. As such, if I can provide the Sentients a perfect means of transportation across any and all distances, I can help push even the most advanced of them further down the path of similarity to our kind.

As a being of Time, merely existing in the Second Realm creates endless paradoxes. However, in dwelling on the subject, I believe I have gleaned a keen insight on the mechanics of travel.

When my kind enters the Second Realm, we possess the ability to travel nearly instantaneously across any distance. Having true form, which is a necessity to enter the Second Realm, comes with certain restrictions. Distance, of course, is a manifestation of Space, one that does not exist in the realm of Aeveaternity. In our realm, we exist across all points of reality at once, because reality happens at every point simultaneously. In the Second Realm, we continue to exist in such a way, though our existence is restricted by linearity. However, unlike all other beings, we can *be* anywhere in the universe at any point, if we simply borrow from the next moment in that linearity. We can travel across all of Space because, in that next moment, we would have already been there.

The complexities of this took me far longer to comprehend than I care to admit, and would not have been possible without the insight of Calara Voya. As a being comprised, at least partially, of Space, she understands the intermingling of the Second Realm and the Aeveaternity in a unique manner. She described it to me as such:

"Imagine a Sentient walking down a long hallway. Now, imagine that Sentient is wearing a cloak. If that cloak were to snag on a nail, the cloak would begin to unravel as the Sentient walked down the hallway, until it was nothing but a single, long string. In essence, that garment would exist at every point down the hallway, but would appear as a single point of that long string.

"We, uncle, as beings of Time, are complete, even if we are stretched into an infinitely long string down the hallway of time, because we are beings unbound by linear reality. You already exist across all points of time, so you can borrow from the next point in the 'string', where you would already be, in order to move instantly to any point in space."

It is still difficult for me to understand the magnitude of linear causality. However, it is a mystery I am determined to one day solve, as it is necessary to the essence of my work.

Based on Calara Voya's understanding, we have created a prototype device that utilizes the principles of movement that she had described. She was absolutely instrumental in not only the conceptualization, but the design and specifications as well. Her skill in these areas has improved with remarkable speed. Whether or not this prototype can be safely applied to the Sentients and their Spatial biology will require more study, however.

Calara Voya and I intend to test this new device with an exceedingly high degree of caution before allowing even a single Sentient to use it. I do not yet fully understand why, but the device seems to leverage something within the Second Realm I have not before encountered—a foundational power that lies underneath the fabric of that existence…

What mysteries has Father hidden even from us? How I miss his presence.

-32-

A foundational power.
Something below the surface…

How I miss father.

Eleva Prime II

I had a visit from the wonderful Calara Voya today. She has a charming habit of sneaking into my workshop—charming, I should say, only because it is Calara doing it. Whether by intention or subconscious, as my abilities have burgeoned, and my tools connect more to my essence, I have become increasingly secretive of my process. I have caught myself quite a bit more displeased when I am unexpectedly interrupted by one of my siblings.

I happened to be working on a new means to aid in Sentient Elevation when I realized she was with me. I cannot accurately guess how long she had been observing me before I noticed her presence, but sufficed to say, she is Viserum's daughter through and through.

Though she shares many of her father's abilities, I have, however, noticed a great divergence between their personalities. Perhaps it is a matter of age, perhaps a matter of her unique constitution, but where her father is a staunch observer—and nothing more—she is filled with wide-eyed and unbridled curiosity.

She has an appreciation for my work, beyond the outcome itself, but in the ideation and creation process—an infinitely endearing attribute. I quite enjoy having her sit with me while I tinker. Save for myself and Father, she likely has a greater understanding of how my inventions work than anyone else, much to the dismay of my siblings. For whatever reason, some have become increasingly intrusive into my workings.

Recently, Calara Voya has even helped me solve a few problems whose solutions had been escaping me for far too long. I believe her unique perspective comes from her connection to both realms. She has a loving touch, something my empathic objects respond quite well to.

Sometimes it is only the joy I sense from them that notifies me that Calara, their cousin, is even in the room.

Aeveaternity Io

In Father's absence, most of our time is spent nurturing the Second Realm in its burgeoning growth. Though the work is rewarding, I know it has taken its toll on my siblings. I myself have noticed my increasing isolation as I work, a separation from my siblings' essence that I had not perceived until now. My work, such as it is, pales in comparison to the duties of the other; I can only begin to imagine the isolation felt by those with even more exposure to the Second Realm than I have.

Father's absence has underscored a characteristic of our design that I had never before appreciated. We twelve were created as part of one whole. Each of us was not only a facet of Father, but, as the children of Time, we were formed to exist and work as one unity. As we have grown into ourselves, into distinct beings, we have also grown apart. This is an effect that has most certainly been amplified by our work with the Second Realm; interacting with Space has pushed us toward form and linearity.

As such, Dignis has requested I make a haven where we may share in each others' presence, and borrow each others' powers to safely touch the Second Realm without risk of exertion, taxation, or, as Raysh might say, contamination.

I believe this to be a brilliant idea, and am determined to make this haven my greatest creation yet.

It will be beautiful even to Viserum's gaze, as elegant in its execution as Serenya's tapestry, and practical enough in use to please even Raysh Io.

Each and every one of us will have an equal place in this haven. It will be designed to amplify and soothe the unique abilities and personalities of my beloved siblings, while giving homage to our collective nature. I will make it a safe nexus point to the Second Realm, accessible only through our combined might so that the effects of the Second Realm do not seep into our own. Every conceivable detail will have my utmost attention.

It will be a testament to Father's request: a balance between the Second Realm and our own. A place where we have form, but are still children of Time.

Perhaps, I think, this balance is the potential I was created to form. Not this haven, but this idea, is a step toward my true purpose.

-35-

Balance, beauty, how noble these goals. To think how far we have striven in their pursuit.

The Spatial Realm 1

I believe I've impressed even Raysh Io, which is no simple feat indeed. For longer than I care to recall, Dignis has been convinced that not only can we, but it is our duty to Elevate the Sentients to our realm of existence. He believes the limitless potential that Father has placed within them can be unlocked with the proper effort, challenge, and guidance. We have already seen incredible leaps in evolution between many Sentient species as a direct impact of our custody, and we have no reason to believe there would be a boundary to that growth. It stands to reason that, with enough time, the Sentients could shed their mortal forms and ascend into beings such as ourselves. Calara Voya herself may even be evidence of the next step in their potential evolution.

If Dignis is correct, if we can achieve this incredible feat, we will not have only given a tremendous gift to all Sentient kind, we will have successfully brought the balance that Father has asked of us. Every Sentient born will Elevate to our realm. The Second Realm will be at a state of perpetual life and ascension, with all who inhabit it following the same path. Chaos and order will be in perfect harmony, as the Sentients yearn to achieve a difficult goal, but one of the utmost meaning. I cannot think of a more noble and worthwhile pursuit.

I have toiled with a way to help Dignis in this quest for some time, and I may have finally done it. Though, I would be remiss if I did not properly share the credit.

In my endless research, I discovered yet another of Father's secrets—he seems to be quite fond of having hidden more mysteries than time, or ability, would allow one to discover.

As per usual, the universe he left us is perfectly ordered, if only we have eyes to see it. Just as he created our realm, a place of pure Time, there exists a realm that is the equal and opposite: a realm of pure Space. The Second Realm, I've come to learn, is the mediation between these two places.

This Spatial realm is difficult for me to understand. It is so far removed from what I am, that it pains me to even dwell on its existence. However, for the purpose of these journals, I shall attempt to explain the Spatial realm, and what I have discovered of its use.

The description of its functionality can best be explained by what Dignis had originally requested of me. He had asked me to "*develop a series of tests and challenges that we could control, in order to push Sentients to their utmost limits—to help them elevate to our plane.*" I am not Father, I cannot read the hearts and minds of every Sentient, and could not possibly know what challenges they would need in order to become like us.

The Spatial realm, however, interacts with reality differently than we do. It is almost empathic in its nature, a trait that admittedly is not present in most of my siblings. I had never thought about the source of my inventions' empathic abilities—I had always assumed their empathic nature was my doing, my own design. Perhaps, in giving form to my inventions, in giving form to anything, I borrowed something from the realm of Space. I may have tapped into a source of power I did not know existed, even if only for inspiration. I have come to consider that maybe our realm is a place of pure potential, whereas the Spatial realm is one of pure existence. My duty, as I've understood it, has been to bring potential into existence. Have I been bringing this existence into our realm with every tool I have made for my siblings, with every attempt I have made to ease their burdens? Is a part of me connected to the Spatial realm in a way that my siblings are not?

I do not know if my discovery of this place was an accident or preordained, but I continue to be astonished by the sheer volume of that which I do not yet understand.

From what I have studied, the Spatial realm is a place of infinite nothingness, until inhabited, at which point it becomes anything and everything. It is in every sense of the word, the opposite to our realm. Where the Aeveaternity exists as every moment at once, simultaneously and yet across all of time, the Spatial realm extends infinitely while also being entirely malleable. I do not claim to comprehend *how* it works, but I have observed what happens when a being of Space-Time interacts with this place. I have known since their inception that a piece of the Sentients is connected intimately to our realm; it stands to reason that a part of them belongs to the Spatial realm as well. It is this connection, I believe, that allows this place of Space-Time to understand the Sentients, read them, look deeply into who they are and change itself accordingly.

My hypothesis is that if a Sentient were to enter this place, and were to conquer it, to emerge from it intact and expel its influence from within him or her, that Sentient would have dominance over that part of his or her being. With such dominance over the Spatial nature of their existence, the Sentients would be far closer to becoming like us, and Elevating to the realm of Aeveaternity.

The Elevated 11

After delivering a gift to Dignis, he began asking curious questions. I had thought nothing of creating an instrument to help him locate Sentients of particular exceptionalities; he's always had a keen interest in that subject matter. I had originally assumed it was to further his pursuit in his work with the Elevated.

His questions, however, centered around the nature of our universe. He was curious about the Second Realm and what I have learned about the realm of pure Space, topics he has historically been disinterested in. He asked, or rather tried to avoid asking, how the Second Realm had been formed, what power maintained it, and whether that power could be found within the Sentients.

To the others, perhaps his queries would have seemed innocent. In fact, the questions were seemingly nonsensical on their face. However, for too long it has been my privilege to study under and with my siblings, and to learn and understand how things work so that I may think through what is possible to what might be.

In the past, if anyone were to pose the same sorts of questions to Dignis, his answer simply would have been 'Father's will'. Why then would he ask me, of all his siblings, the intricate details of Father's greatest creation, as if he were searching for something Father had hidden.

Of all of us, he would be the last I would have expected to question such things.

The Spatial Realm II

To date we have seen many Sentients successfully emerge from the Spatial realm. However, we have yet to see a Sentient Elevate as a result of it. Though these Sentients continue to achieve greater feats than any in history, it does not seem to be enough.

The Spatial realm has proven invaluable in forging incredibly complete and fulfilled Sentients in every sense of the term. Regardless of this fact, the series of trials presented to them in the Spatial realm, as thorough as they are, is not the final step in fully Elevating to our plane of existence—that much has become abundantly clear.

Even still, Dignis has begun to make completion of these tests a central tenant of the Sentients who follow his specific guidance. The fervour with which the Sentients have begun to venerate my siblings is its own matter of concern. It is bordering nearly on worship.

In any case, Dignis is insistent we continue to use the Spatial realm as a method to help the Sentients Elevate. It, more than anything else, has pushed this goal forward. I suppose he is correct…

The Spatial Realm…
what is its purpose?

What do we not yet know?

The Spatial Realm III

I feel a shame I have never encountered in my long life. I fear Dignis asks too much, he is too loyal of a son for his own good. Though I warned him that my original hypothesis of the Spatial realm's effect on Elevation has proven false, I should have known it would take tragedy to dissuade him.

How many innocent souls must be lost to the eternity of the Spatial realm? We now know with certainty that only the most profoundly readied souls should even attempt to face the horrors of that realm. By all available evidence, failure, to be trapped in that realm for all of eternity, is a fate far worse than what the Sentients refer to as death. The Sentients that have made it through have reported experiencing time differently in that realm; some have claimed it felt like decades had passed, while only truly being inside for days. Those that successfully emerge, though changed for the better, have not been able to Elevate. If that is the case, why do we continue these experiments?

No one dares to utter the words aloud, but there is a growing seed of doubt as to whether a Sentient can truly become like us.

I can sense a divide forming within Dignis. He places the blame for this failure solely on himself. He believes so strongly that Elevating the Sentients is the ultimate means to fulfill Father's wish, yet every attempt has proven ill-fated. "*Millions of generations of Sentients and only marginal improvements to show for it,*" were his exact words.

I too feel deeply responsible, though not because I expect the Sentients to Elevate. In fact, I am exceedingly proud of the progress their many species have made, considering how vastly spread they are across the universe, and the relatively minute time they have in their mortal lives. No, I place blame on myself for opening a door to the Spatial realm without considering the consequences deeply enough.

Even worse, we have no means of attempting to retrieve anyone who is lost to that place. Were myself or my siblings to enter that realm, the very essence of our beings would be ripped apart.

I must think harder for a solution to this problem. For now, I will devise a means of closing off the portals to the Spatial realm, save for those who have proven their readiness. I believe this is a compromise Dignis and the others will be willing to abide.

The Spatial Realm IV

All attempts to retrieve the lost Sentients have failed. There is no way to know how long those who have entered the Spatial realm and not yet emerged will be trapped there, or how long it will seem to them.

My siblings and I have no way to truly understand what happens in that realm, save for the accounts given to us from the Sentients who have made it through. However, their minds can only interpret so much, and they are beings of a different nature than our own. Their experiences and perspectives do not map well onto how we, as children of Time, interpret the universe.

We have tried sending those who have successfully emerged from the Spatial realm back in to retrieve their lost brethren, but they are simply met with more tests when they re-enter. By its nature and design, the Spatial realm is an unnavigable labyrinth.

I refuse to give up on attempting to save those who are lost. I am working on a device to peer into the realm. Maybe, if we can locate them…

The prototype takes a tremendous amount of power to operate. Viserum exhausted his abilities using it only briefly. He's always been opposed to our meddling. Though, I can sense his true sincerity and concern in the matter of retrieving these lost souls.

The Aevea IX

I am of two minds.

Father's absence has begun to take a noticeable toll on my siblings and myself. We all feign to one another as though we are unaffected, but I can sense otherwise. I have studied under each of my siblings for too long not to notice a difference in their behaviour. Whether they realize the change in themselves, however, is an entirely different matter.

I am not who I used to be. I struggle to pull away from my workshop, even when following Dignis' guidance to do so.

Even in my own musings, I have become increasingly focused on my inventions, nearly obsessively.

These journals have helped me keep track of the passage of events. Reading them to myself, I can see a burgeoning pattern.

My purpose, my responsibility, has become all consuming. I, at least, have the respite of my dear niece. My siblings, for the most part, have never been able to form connections in this way. If I am so deeply impacted by the absence of Father's guidance, the effect must be multiple-fold for my brothers and sisters.

Was this Father's intention? Is there a lesson to be learned even in this struggle?

The power of connection.

My savior or my downfall?

The Elevated III

I believe Dignis has come to realize that, despite all attempts, the Sentients cannot Elevate to our level of being in a way that we can immediately control. Given the growth and potential I know to be within them, I do believe that over time this may be an accomplishable feat. However, in an act of what Dolour would refer to as irony, it appears that Dignis has become discouraged by the prospect of the passage of time. For beings such as ourselves, the difference between a few hundred or a few billion generations of Sentients should be of no consequence. Perhaps we've been overly involved in the happenings of the Second Realm for too long.

I have studied the Sentients and their incredible variety across the universe. Many have made amazing leaps so far beyond where they have started, it is nearly miraculous to consider. The inhabitants across the entire planet of Verakc have honed tremendous empathic abilities, on par with even my most inspired inventions. Some species of Sentients have developed means to change their form, even to survive in the harshest of environments without protection. Nearly all who follow the path of Elevation have strengthened their innate tether to our realm, and yet… none so far have proven they can become what we are. What they have proven, however, is that we do not yet know the limits of their abilities, and that even we still have much to learn.

Viserum and Serenya have, in their own ways, confirmed that as the Sentients walk the path of Elevation, they do in fact transform the essence of their being. From my understanding, the Sentients are not so much changing who they are, as they are heightening those traits already innate to them. This, of course, explains, at least in part, the incredible leaps and variation in Sentients' abilities across cultures and worlds.

Even still, though he refuses to show it outwardly, Dignis is becoming ever more disconcerted. As an increasing number of promising Sentients inevitably perish to age, he is slowly becoming more stoic. Whether it is a burgeoning empathic ability in myself, or a lifetime of studying my brother, I can tell his expressions are hardening over time. Dignis wishes for nothing more than for the Sentients to become like us—perfect stewards of Father's will—the ultimate keepers of balance, as he refers to us.

I, however, believe that they have a different destiny. The Sentients are of the nature to live and to die. This nature, these limits, are part of the gift that Father has given them, a gift that we do not share. As such, we were created with different, but not superior gifts, and our duty to Father is different, and not superior.

I know it is difficult for my brothers and sisters to understand death, or even what it means for something to end. They do not see how finality can create purpose—after all, we were all given our purpose directly from Father himself.

Alas, I am troubled. Not because I feel we are mistreating or misguiding the Sentients, in fact, I believe the opposite to be true. I do think that Dignis' aim is noble, and indeed is part of what Father intended for us. As time passes, I realize that Father's instructions were far more nuanced than any of us could have understood. Then again, I, unlike my siblings, have developed an intimate relationship with the passage of time, and have become prone to change.

This revelation is concerning. If I am correct, I do not know what this truth might do to Dignis.

The Aevea x

I went to see Dignis today. He was pacing his great chamber. "*Balance…*
our duty is to create balance." He was repeating this over and over. They
were reminiscent of Father's final words to us. Am I misremembering, or
is he? Was it not "*…to maintain balance?*"

<u>*Memory*</u> *– an interesting*
dilemma for beings such as
us.

Project Aesceplii

I've begun research on what I hope will be a purely scientific endeavor. Though most words contained in these pages are meant to record my thoughts, these entries are meant to remind me exactly why I felt it necessary to start this research.

I know now that there is a realm that is equal and opposite in power to our own. The question then becomes, might Father have also created beings with powers equal and opposite to our own?

The power of Space is likely one I will never truly comprehend, but I do not have the ability to rid myself of this question.

Just as we exert our influence on the Second Realm, the Spatial realm does the same. After all, the Sentients are beings of form, of time and space, of cause and effect. I have seen this bond in the eons that I have studied them, served them, crafted for them my children so that we both may grow. I do not know if that is the reason they have not yet been able to Elevate, and frankly that is not my current concern.

What I do seek is a counterbalance to the tremendous gifts Father has granted my siblings, and myself. I can no longer deny the shift in perspective amongst my siblings. They speak about the Sentients and the Second Realm as if it were not a creation of Father's, but a burden to be dealt with. I cannot predict what this change might eventually mean, but predicting the future has never been my role.

All I can be certain of is that the passage of time has indeed changed my brothers and sisters, and I must be prepared for any eventuality.

For now, I intend to keep this project secret, away from prying eyes. Until I make significant progress, I shall refer to it only as Project Aesceplii.

Project Aesceplü 11: Fire

FIRE.

It is immaculate. Joyous, pure, but far from simple.

I have faced more impasses in my research for this project, ones leaving me without any sense of next steps, than I have in my entire existence. I have stretched my mind well beyond anything I have done before, but finally, I have made progress.

After endless searching—and I must emphasize that this was an act of searching, not one of invention—the solution came to me. I am certain that this creature allowed me to discover it, allowed me to contain its essence in an incarnate form. I believe that, for whatever reason, this creature has decided to trust me, it has sensed within me my intentions, and believes them to be true. The fact that it chose to be found, that my searching drew it to me, is an important distinction; it is one that must be recorded for the sake of accuracy.

Warm, brilliant, cunning, and the embodiment of passion. It came into being in a larval, or, perhaps I should say, infant, form—but a fraction of its near limitless power. It has contained itself in a body that is entirely unassuming, and replete with far more potential than one would assume for a foundational building block of an entire realm of existence. Is this form my influence, or a design of its own brilliance?

My sincere hope, if I have done my work correctly, is that it has taken this shape because it has not yet found its chosen other half: a Sentient whom it believes epitomizes the necessary traits to be deserving of its partnership.

Though I do not dare think I have the power to create a being of Space, I must give myself credit for the process by which this deeply ephemeral being has taken form. I have finally learned, through a great deal of time, failure, and struggle, that the purpose of my creation was to help Father bridge the divide between Space and Time. I believe this melding of Space and Time is the balance of which Father spoke. Of course, Father had started that bridge so long ago in his creation of the Second Realm and the Sentients. And it is *through* the Sentients, through their connection to all three realms, that the Elemental Building Blocks of Space, as I have called them, shall take form.

I should note that while I have been diligent in recording my efforts throughout my life, I shall never put to words the detailed process that has finally brought this ambition into reality. Perhaps that omission is an act of heresy for one such as myself, but the purpose of this project is far too important to risk its success on my own hubris. For that matter, I am not so vain as to think myself able to predict this creature's true and final form, or whom it would deem its equal.

For now, I shall take solace in the fact that I have helped bring about something well beyond the ken of my brothers and sisters.

Project Aesceplü III: Air

What an enjoyable process it was to form this Elemental Building Block. Like playing with a jubilant child, it moved toward and away from me with such energetic frivolity. I feel like I have been given life and purpose anew through this effort.

Movement: I believe that is the essence of this creature's abilities. The spirit and levity of all things in the universe, incarnated in the form of "air." I imagine whoever this creature bonds with will be unshakeably true, and, I do not doubt, wholeheartedly willful.

I continue to learn more about these creatures as I refine the method of giving them form. Truly, I am not certain if it is I or them who is leading the process in the end. How can I have lived so long and still have so much more to learn?

My siblings... the path that they walk down is one I simply cannot follow. I refuse to believe that what they are attempting to do is the purpose for which Father created us. Of course, none will admit what I believe to be the truth, but I must take precautions to prevent the worst.

I have watched them change, and while that change has been slow, in writing and reading these journals, I can so clearly see their decline. Serenya's hands have become sharp, Dignis' shoulders stern, Viserum's eyes dull, and most others have become but dark shadows of themselves.

I must finish my work, and I must keep it hidden at all costs. I will not raise arms against my siblings, but I will not betray Father's final request simply to spare them.

The forming of every proceeding Elemental, as I've taken to calling them, changes me in a profound manner. I did not truly understand this until I encountered the Elemental of Water.

As it relates to the physical and metaphysical characteristics of the Sentients, I believe this one would be connected to what most of the Sentient philosophies refer to as the 'soul'—the inimitable, arguably unchangeable, part of the Sentients that fundamentally differentiates them from one another. It is an invisible kernel, buried deep within; it is the incorporeal foundation upon which life is built. I am not sure if this is what Serenya refers to when she discusses the threads that connect the Sentients to our realm, or the colours that Viserum sees when he looks at the Sentients, although I do not believe it to be the exact same concept.

I have never encountered a power similar to this. It is divine, and yet unique. It is all and infinitely divisible. Touching it, I feel close to Father, while also mournful of his absence. I feel the deep and intense connection it has to all other 'souls', almost as though it is the source of connection itself. More than any of the Elementals I have come into contact with, this one makes me feel alone, not because loneliness is in its nature, but simply because it has forced me to reflect on my own existence.

This Elemental is exceedingly powerful, but perhaps the most unstable of the four building blocks I intend to form.

I suspect that whoever it chooses to bond with will be an intensely complex individual, perhaps even unique amongst the others. I expect it to seek out a companion of powerful and true depth of character. However, if my assumptions are correct, and things progress as they have been, I will never see this for myself...

The soul. The undercurrent of the Sentient experience. If only I could...

Project Aesceplüv:
Air

The Elemental Building Block of Air was the first to go dormant. This is an unexpected, though I believe, entirely positive turn of events.

In its dormant form, the Elemental has reverted to a shell of stone. Though I can sense its phenomenal power, it is a mere fraction of a fraction of its strength in even its larval state. I believe this reversion is due to its lack of connection to a Sentient partner. I expect something similar to happen to the Elemental of Fire shortly, even though I personally feel a bond to the creature—one I was not expecting to form.

I have labeled this dormant form a Calix, and will refer to it as such moving forward. The more labels and layers of secrecy I can create around my work here, the safer it will be for everyone.

It stands to reason that even from within the Calix, this Elemental is exerting the same level of influence on the Second Realm as when it was awakened. I firmly believe that the forms these Elementals are taking are but incidental to their impact and nature. As beings of Space, the Elementals are beings *of* form. Unlike us, the state in which they exist does not seem to impair their behaviour or abilities. They existed before my interference to solidify them, though not in such a manner as to limit the plans of my brothers and sisters.

Even still, I will put every manner of protection that I can upon all of the Calia. My hope is that these wonderful beings will never have to be awakened. If I fulfill my plan correctly, they never will be.

Project Aesceplü v1: Earth

My work is nearly complete.

I have nothing but regret about what will inevitably come to pass, but I see no other path forward. It is difficult for me to believe what we have become in Father's absence, but I can no longer deny the truth. Diplomacy and planning have never been my strength, perhaps if they were, I could have prevented what is to come.

This fourth and final safeguard, the one that is most deeply bound to the Spatial realm, has changed me, as the other three have. It is grounded, strong, firm, and compelled most certainly by cause and effect. It is form incarnate, the opposite of ephemeral. It is the body, the embodiment that contains the potential. In many ways, it is memory itself—the solidified form of time. It is so far beyond the comprehension of a creature like myself, that even when looking upon it I have become something new.

I understand now what Dolour has known since our creation. I can feel the passage of time. Though I am still made in the image that Father had intended, I have become something my brothers and sisters will not recognize, something they will never willfully understand.

They intend to do something truly terrible in their misguided pursuit. I know that now.

I could stop them by force. I could strike them down. I have the power to do so. I have always had that strength. But I refuse. I could never hurt them in such a way. After all, I love my brothers and sisters.

*If I knew then, if I looked
deeper, could I have changed...
anything?*

My Dearest Calara

My dearest Calara,

How your father hates when I refrain from using your full name.

To you, I leave everything, should you wish to inherit it.

While my life's work was in giving form to wonders that I have come to consider my children, and though I am but merely an uncle, I hope you know that I think of you as closer to me than anyone or anything, save for Father himself.

I believe it is the deep connection to the Second Realm and its inhabitants that I have forged over so many years that has given me a unique ability amongst my siblings—one that was shared, perhaps, only by your father. I feel that I have learned the ability to love.

Though by the time you read this, I will likely be gone, know that I love you more than I have words to say. I trust no one but you with the secrets of my work. And, my dear Calara, for as close as we are, there is much I have not yet told you for your own safety, and even more that I simply did not have time to share.

What you must know is that the truth to all that I have learned is hidden within my writing. Of the countless pursuits I have given my time to, I consider my journals to be amongst the most important. My writings have done more than turn thought into history. While they will provide you with an understanding of the functionality of many of my inventions, they serve a far greater purpose: they record my growth into what I believe Father had always intended me to become.

This book is the key to the many secrets I have hidden, if you wish to find them. In my numerous other journals, you will learn of many inventions, ideas, things that never came to pass, and things I was foolish enough to have brought into existence. I ask nothing of you, other than to look beyond the surface, if seeking those tomes is a path you choose to follow. If, on the other hand, you wish to let those secrets rest for all of Aeveaternity, I will be equally as proud.

I have placed upon my writings protections that will ensure only you, and whoever you deem worthy, are capable of discovering them, let alone reading them. Through these words, and the trust we share, I hope you understand why I needed to do what I have done. If, in reading all that I have chronicled, you are able to see a flaw in my thinking, I pray only that, if faced with a similar circumstance, you will have the tools to avoid my chosen fate.

You, and you alone, are the steward of my creations now, just as we were supposed to be the stewards of Father's. Though I do not dare compare myself to him, I do think perhaps I can understand a fraction of the pain he would feel if my brothers and sisters enacted their plan.

There is more to learn; there will always be more to learn, more unknown than we can ever know. Even for a being of Time, we will never live long enough to have learned all that there is, and *that* is an incredible gift. It means that there is always more to do, always more potential to be given form, if only we have the willingness to seek it out. Understanding that final lesson, more so than any invention, made me feel that my life had purpose.

I love you as if you were my own. Stay safe, my dearest Calara.

Though I may never see that insatiable hunger for knowledge in your eyes again, it is through your eyes that I will live on. Just remember, knowledge is never a replacement for wisdom.

Your ever faithful uncle,

Paschia

I leave it all to you,
Calara.

Acknowledgements

Thank you to all the alpha readers, beta readers, and friends and family who gave me feedback on this story. This was an experiment that (I hope) went right, thanks to all of your input.

A very special thank you to my friend, Adrian M. Gibson. His interior design work turned this novella from a story into a work of art.

If you like this story, please consider leaving a review on Amazon, Goodreads, or wherever else reviews exist. It really helps get the story in front of more people.

If you want to read more in the series, all of the other books are available on Amazon as well as www.elementsoftime.ca.

About the Author

Sam Paisley was born and raised in Toronto, Ontario, Canada, where he lives with his wife, dog, and daughter-on-the-way.

Driven by a lifelong passion for storytelling, Sam has made it his mission as an author to create worlds and stories that bring joy and escapism to others. He was raised on a healthy diet of TV, movies, music and pop-culture of the 80s, 90s, and 2000s, and he does his absolute best to sneak in easter eggs to his inspirations whenever he can.

If you like his work, want to learn more about The Elements of Time series, or find additional content beyond the books, please visit www.element-softime.ca.